Arlyn of the Forest

by

Mairiis Kilcher

Written by Mairiis Kilcher   Artwork by Mairiis Kilcher

Graphic Design by Joy

This book belongs to
this very special person

Name: _____

The adventures in this story
are dedicated to my son,
Arlyn Davidson

In his heart,
he will forever be
a child of the forest.

Arlyn lives with his mother and father in a wild enchanting forest of Alaska.

He has many friends.
From sunrise to sunset, he is never lonely.

At the break of dawn
he is already out of the house.

Good morning trees! Good morning squirrels!

I brought some corn for you to eat!

He meets mother moose on the way.
Her calf is curious about Arlyn.

The little hares are curious too!

The varied thrushes are singing from the spruce tops. Arlyn knows where one thrush nest is hidden.

There is a place in the alders where he can watch the fox sparrows scratch up old leaves in search of grubs.

Each morning Arlyn goes to the cliff to see how the baby eagles are growing.

Mother spruce hen is very upset.
One chick is missing!

But Arlyn finds it in the deep grass
and brings it home to safety.

Now it is time to run home
and feed the chickens.
Arlyn has some flowers for Mother.
She is already fixing breakfast.

Father is out chopping wood.

The chickens are excited!

Here comes Arlyn with a special treat!

"Good morning pigeons!
How are my favorite birds today?"

They flock around him while he gathers
the chicken eggs.

Arlyn has some grain for the farm animals.

Far away, Arlyn hears a bell.

He runs along the pasture trails until he finds the horse grazing in her favorite pasture by the ocean.

He rides her bareback through tangled thickets and mysterious, hidden meadows.

Whoa! There is a hole in
that dead cottonwood tree!

A woodpecker nest!

In another tree he sees a strange
shape. A magpie nest?

He climbs up to investigate.

Sure enough!
The most beautiful magpie eggs!

Arlyn checks to see if swallows are living in the bird houses that Father helped him build.

Mother gave him some corn to feed the steller jays. They are very tame.

The ermine looks hungry too.

Goodbye, Mother! I am going back
to the forest to see what I can see.

I will bring you some mushrooms for supper.

Suddenly from a high ridge comes
the sharp yelping of a coyote.
Arlyn tries calling him.

Will the coyote answer?

The coyote does not reply.
He is very shy and cautious.
Arlyn tries to get closer.

But the coyote runs away.

But first he tries calling the coyote once more. "Yip yip yip yay-ooooo!"

There is no answer from the coyote.

Arlyn is picking wild mushrooms.

The coyote is very curious.
He comes a little closer to watch.

Arlyn sits very still as a nuthatch flies down to land on his hand.

Evening is coming.
Slowly Arlyn is on his way home.

Arlyn goes by the lake to see if his ducks and geese are coming home.

A black bear watches from a distant hill.

They follow Arlyn back to the
barnyard for the night.

While Mother is frying
the mushrooms for supper,
Arlyn goes down to the pasture
to see if all the animals are ok.

They look happy.

The chickens are already
on their roost for the night.

Arlyn goes to say goodnight
to the forest creatures.

The owl calls to Arlyn from an old tree,
"Hoo-hoo-hoo!"

Hop, hop! This hare looks wide awake.
He seems to be in a big hurry!

Perhaps the coyote is nearby?

Arlyn gives a long, loud coyote cry.

And from his favorite high hill
the coyote answers!
Soon he and Arlyn are calling
back and forth to each other.

The spruce chicks look safe
and warm, huddled under
their mother's wings for the night.

In the moonlit meadow,
Arlyn sees mother moose and her calf
browsing on willow shoots.

With night, the forest grows quieter.

The squirrel is sleeping curled up in his cozy nest of dry ferns.

In his favorite ferny hollow, Arlyn listens every evening to the songs of the Hermit Thrush.

"Yoo - hoo! Arlyn! Come home!"
Mother is calling for supper.

And then it is time for bed.

Arlyn's day has come to an end.

What will the new sunrise bring
for Arlyn and his friends ?

Thanks to all the many special people for their enthusiastic support in making this book possible.

Made in the USA
Middletown, DE
26 September 2023